W9-AVR-594

The subject matter and vocabulary have been selected with expert assistance, and the brief and simple text is printed in large, clear type.

Children's questions are anticipated and facts presented in a logical sequence. Where possible, the books show what happened in the past and what is relevant today.

Special artwork has been commissioned to set a standard rarely seen in books for this reading age and at this price.

Full-colour illustrations are on all 48 pages to give maximum impact and provide the extra enrichment that is the aim of all Ladybird Leaders.

A Ladybird Leader

dinosaurs

Written by Colin Douglas
Illustrated by B. H. Robinson

Ladybird Books Loughborough

At first, nothing lived on the land or in the sea.

There were no plants, no animals,
no people.

Life began in the sea

Trilobite
(Try-lo-bite)

Sponges

Life began in the sea.
The first living things
were very, very small.
Some grew into tiny worms.

Belemnite

Jellyfish

Ammonite

Starfish

Later, there were jellyfish, starfish and sponges.

Later still, there were living things that had shells.

7

The Age of Fishes

Dinichthys
(Din-*ik*-this)
30 feet (9.14 m)
long

Pteraspis
(Tair-*as*-pis)
6 inches (152 mm) long

Fish like these
began to live in the sea.
Some were very small.
Some were as long as a bus.

At this time, plants began to grow
on the land.

Some were like ferns.

There were even tall trees.

Some fish crawled onto the land

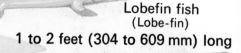

Lobefin fish
(Lobe-fin)
1 to 2 feet (304 to 609 mm) long

The world became a drier place.
Many rivers and lakes dried up.
Some fish had very strong fins.
They could crawl onto the land
with these.

The first amphibians (am-fib-y-ans)

Ichthyostega
(Ik-*thee-oh*-steega)
3 feet (914 mm) long

After millions of years,
some fish grew legs and had lungs.
They had become amphibians.
Amphibians can live on land
and in the water.

A larger amphibian

Eryops
(*Air*-ee-ops)
5 feet (1.52 m) long

This larger amphibian lived
in the warm swamps.

A swamp is a place where water
and mud collect.

A very large amphibian

Eogyrinus
(Ee-oh-*jigh*-rine-us)

The very large amphibian on this page
was more than 15 feet (4.57 m) long.

Some amphibians were only
2 inches (50 mm) long.

The first reptiles

Seymouria
(See-*more*-ee-ya)
2 feet (609 mm) long

Slowly, some amphibians
changed into reptiles.
This may have been
one of the first reptiles.

Edaphosaurus
(Ee-*daf*-oh-sawrus)
9 feet (2.74 m) long

This fin-backed reptile ate plants.

Reptiles lay their eggs on land.

Amphibians lay their eggs in water.

Another fin-backed reptile

Dimetrodon
(Di-*meet*-ro-don)
9 feet (2.74 m) long

Dimetrodon ate flesh, not plants.
It probably ate amphibians.

An amphibian and a reptile of today

Frog

Alligator

The frog is an amphibian.
It lays its eggs in the water.
An alligator is a reptile.
It lays its eggs on land.

Sea reptiles

Ichthyosaurus
(*Ik*-thee-oh-sawrus)
7 to 30 feet (2.13 to 9.14 m) long

Some reptiles went back to live
all the time in the water.

The females did not lay eggs on land.

The eggs hatched inside the females.

Plesiosaurus
(*Ples*-y-oh-sawrus)

Some plesiosaurs were more than
40 feet (12.19 m) long.

They had very long necks.

Their long necks helped
when catching fish.

Gliding reptiles

Wing span:
about 1 foot (304 mm)

Pterodactylus
(Tair-oh-*dak*-till-us)

Some reptiles grew wings.
The largest had
a wing span of 27 feet (8.23 m).
Some were no larger than
a small bird.

Wing span: about 4 feet
(1.21 m)

Dimorphodon
(Die-*more-foe*-don)

Rhamphorhynchus
(Ram-for-*rink*-us)

Wing span: about 3 feet (914 mm)

These reptiles probably glided.
They did not fly like birds.

More about gliding reptiles

Gliding reptiles did not have feathers
on their wings.

Their wings were made of skin.

They ate fish or small reptiles
and insects.

Pteranodon
(Tair-*an*-oh-don)
Wing span:
about 25 feet
(7.62 m)

Footprints from the past

In America, monster footprints
were found about 150 years ago.

Later, some very large bones were found

A skeleton was built up with these bones

A monster skeleton

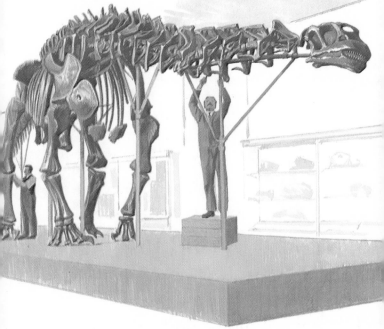

Skeleton of Brontosaurus

The footprints were those of a dinosaur.
So were the bones.
The word 'dinosaur' means
'terrible lizard'.

Diplodocus and Brontosaurus

There were many kinds of dinosaur.
They lived long before the first men.
Some were very small
and moved quickly.
Others were very big and moved slowly.

Brontosaurus
(*Bron*-toh-sawrus)
65 feet (19.81 m)
long

Diplodocus
(Dip-*plod*-oh-kus)
90 feet (27.43 m) long

The dinosaurs in this picture
were very heavy and slow.
They did not like to fight.
They felt safer in the water.

Stegosaurus moved slowly.
It had huge spikes on its tail.
These ripped into attackers.

Stegosaurus
(*Steg*-oh-sawrus)
20 feet (6.09 m) long

Antrodemus
(An-trow-*dee*-mus)
30 feet (9.14 m) long

Antrodemus hunted other animals.
Its mouth opened so wide
it could swallow small animals whole.
Its back legs were 9 feet (2.74 m) high.

Hypsilophodon and Iguanodon

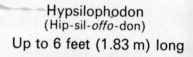

Hypsilophodon
(Hip-sil-*offo*-don)
Up to 6 feet (1.83 m) long

This dinosaur was quite small
and ran quite quickly on two legs.

It probably climbed trees
to get away from its enemies.

Iguanodon
(Ig-*wan*-o-don)
30 feet (9.14 m) long

This one also ate plants and was larger.

It had several rows of teeth.

Each front leg had a bony spike.

This spike was used when fighting.

Polacanthus

Polacanthus
(Pol-a-*kan*-thus)
14 feet (4.27 m) long

The remains of this dinosaur
were found in England.

The double row of spikes on its back
kept other animals away.

Ankylosaurus

Ankylosaurus
(An-*kile*-oh-sawrus)
15 feet (4.57 m) long

This dinosaur had an almost flat body
covered with bony plates.

At the end of its tail
was a big lump of bone with spikes.

The tail was used as a club.

Anatosaurus and Corythosaurus

Anatosaurus
(An-*at*-oh-sawrus)
40 feet (12.19 m) lo

Some dinosaurs had feet like a bird's.
Dinosaurs probably croaked loudly
when they were angry.

Corythosaurus
(*Kor*-ith-oh-sawrus)
30 feet (9.14 m) long

Corythosaurus could swim well.

Remains of it have been found in Canada.

Its name means 'helmet reptile'.

The bony ridge on its head
looks like a helmet.

Protoceratops

(Pro-toe-*sair*-a-tops)
6 feet (1.83 m) long

In 1922, the fossils of eggs like these
were found in Mongolia.

Each egg was about 8 inches
(203 mm) long.

Probably a dinosaur lived
for only 50 years.

Styracosaurus and Tyrannosaurus

Styracosaurus
(Sty-*rak*-oh-sawrus)
15 feet (4.57 m) long

This dinosaur looked fierce
but ate plants, not other animals.

It had a beak like a parrot's

and long spikes on its head.

Tyrannosaurus
(Tie-*ran*-oh-sawrus)
40 feet (12.19 m) long

This was the largest and most dreaded of the flesh-eating dinosaurs.

Its jaw was 4 feet (1.21 m) long and its terrible teeth 6 inches (152 mm) long. 39

Monoclonius and Triceratops

Monoclonius
(Mon-oh-*klon*-ee-us)
20 feet (6.09 m) long

There were dinosaurs
for nearly 150 million years.

Those shown here
were the last of the dinosaurs.

Triceratops
(Try-*sair-a*-tops)
30 feet (9.14 m) long

Triceratops was a very big
and savage fighter.

Its two larger horns were more
than 3 feet (914 mm) long.

The first real birds

Archaeopteryx
(Ark-ee-*op*-ter-ix)

The first real birds lived
at the time of the dinosaurs.

They had feathered wings.

These birds were as big as a crow.

These birds had teeth like
a reptile's.

They had tails like a lizard's.

These were covered with feathers.

The first mammals

Phascolotherium
(Fas-kol-oh-theer-eum)

A mammal is an animal which is fed,
when young, on its mother's milk.

The first mammals lived
at the time of the first birds.

Megatherium
(*Mega*-theer-eum)

The first mammals were
no larger than mice or rats.

Later, the mammals became
much bigger.

This one was 18 feet (5.48 m) high.

More mammals

Uintatherium
(Oo-inta-*theer*-eum)
12 feet (3.66 m) long

This animal was as big as
an elephant.

It looked fierce, but did not
eat other animals.

Baluchitherium
(Bal-oo-chi-*theer*-ium)

This animal was three times as tall
as a man.

It was 27 feet (8.23 m) long and ate
leaves and twigs.

The first horses

Eohippus
(Ee-oh-hip-pus)

The first horse was Eohippus.
It was only **12 inches (304 mm)** high.
It had toes, not hooves.

The woolly rhinoceros
8 feet (2.44 m) long

In the Ice Ages, the world became
very cold.
The woolly rhinoceros lived then.
Its long, hairy coat kept it warm.

The woolly mammoth

By this time, the first men were living.
They painted pictures of this animal
on the walls of their caves.

They killed mammoths for food.

The sabre-toothed tiger

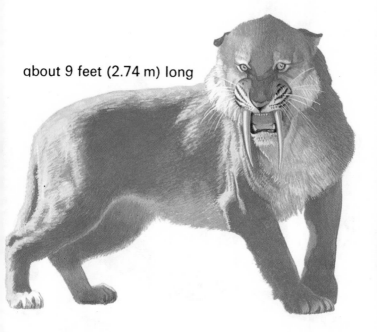

about 9 feet (2.74 m) long

This tiger had front teeth 9 inches
(228 mm) long.

It could kill a mammoth.

SIZES
Compared with man

Present-day Elephant

Mammoth

Stegosaurus

Pteranodo